Joseph and Sons Carpentry, Nazareth

A Story of Jesus' Childhood

For ages 5 to 95

By Leone A Waddell Johnson

I dedicate this book to Reverend Elias and Donna Malki, Devora Moar, all the grandmothers in my life, and Nazareth Village for the inspiration, and especially Becky Ekizian who grew up in Lebanon and encouraged me to write this book as did Charlotte and Joanne Brace, John and Judy Kolb, Nona Hegen, and Judy Dropko. Thank you all, Leone

Pictures, drawings, and artwork - Most of the drawings throughout this book were done by Alyx Christophe from photographs that I took, some were her work alone. The picture of liquid flowing into a clay pot is in this book several times; it is a copy of a painting named Vessels by my artist friend Elaine Neigel from Canada. There are only a couple of prints included from public domain stock.

First American Copyright © October 12, 2018
Second edition: November 9, 2018

ISBN-13: 978-1727874365

ISBN-10: 1727874366

Forward

Helping Leone with this book has been a wonderful and joyful experience. It was a delight to help tease out the details of what life might have been like for Jesus as a young person and portraying Jesus in situations that happen in families and everyday life. I love this book! - Alyx Christophe MSW, MBA

> *During the creative process of writing this book, Alyx added many components, topics, and contents for these stories. I am grateful for the gifts and talents Alyx added to this endeavor. Thank you, your friend Leone*

Prolog

This novel fills in the missing years of Jesus' life as a boy and a young man and shows the human side so often dismissed due to his divinity. It contains many stories as I have imagined what Jesus as a young boy would have experienced and what he would have learned from his earthly Father Joseph.

I challenge you to read the Gospels of Jesus Christ from the beginning of His ministry. I pray that this book will be enjoyed by children of all ages and those of us who have never grown up.

Table of Contents

Title Page	1
Dedication and Acknowledgements	2
Forward	3
Prolog	3
Five Years Old - coming home from Egypt	5
Six - at home in Nazareth	10
Seven - wooden buckets and Galilee	13
Eight - making things	20
Nine - hammer handles and stir sticks	24
Ten - heavenly understanding	28
Eleven - Giant and adventure	32
Twelve - Bar Mitzvah	41
Thirteen - I am now an adult	45
Fourteen - temple dedication	49
Fifteen - the swing	51
Sixteen - balance	53
Seventeen - a new cart	56
Eighteen - Ein Gedi and the Dead Sea	60
Nineteen - the grieving stranger	66
Twenty - the city gates	70
Twenty-one - Za'atar	73
Twenty-two - sandstorm	75
Twenty-three - friends	82
Twenty-four - a cold winter	86
Twenty-five - reminiscing	88
Twenty-six - bed-bags	90
Twenty-seven - the accident	92
Twenty-eight - donkeys, goats, and mayhem	93
Twenty-nine - Joseph is ill	94
Thirty- spending more time teaching	97
Thirty-one - scroll of Isaiah	103
Thirty-two - making wooden chests for my sisters	106
Thirty-three - sister Salome	113
What others thought, Sophie	119
Elise	120
Ann LaGrange	121
Story support	122
Afterward	128
Contact information	129
Boaz and Barley	130

Five Years Old

Hello, my name is Jesus and I am five. People tell me I that I was conceived by the Holy Ghost in Nazareth and was born in Bethlehem in a cave where the animals slept. I am not sure what I think about different people telling me stories of who I am but this one thing I know for sure: I have a Heavenly Father and He is going to guide my spiritual life and my Earthly father is a carpenter and a mason and I will learn how to build things out of wood and stone.

It has been told to me that King Herod killed all the first born males in Bethlehem and if not for an angel appearing to Joseph I would be gone too. The angel told him to take my mother Mary and me to Egypt. Just before we left, a caravan came from afar and the people brought gifts of frankincense, myrrh, and gold. The Heavenly Father sent them and told them to bring gifts worthy of a king. My dad was grateful for the gold that would enable him to care for us in Egypt.

After some time, while we were in Egypt, the angel told Joseph in a dream that old King Herod was dead and we were to move back to the home Joseph had prepared for Mother Mary in Nazareth. On the way back to Nazareth my baby brother and Mother Mary rode the donkey while we walked along side. It was a five day journey and we had very good weather along the way. My baby brother, me and Mother picked flowers and played in the Jordan River. Mother prepared all of the food as well as she could and I liked the dried fish best.

Mom cooked leek soup with the leeks we got in Egypt and I remember Dad telling Mom "don't use all the leeks, we want to plant some in Nazareth."

Mom said it will be good to get home and be with our family and friends again. Dad said there will be a great celebration when they see us coming down the path. There will be singing, dancing, food, and wine and lots of happy greetings. I will get to meet my cousins, aunts, and uncles for the first time!

While coming from Egypt Dad told me the story about Jericho and the walls that tumbled down by people blowing ram's horns seven times. It was a miracle that the walls came down from the horns. Dad also said there are lots of fruits in Jericho that we could buy like oranges, melons, grapefruit, pomegranates, dates, figs, and nuts.

When we got to Jericho the market place was filled with stuff I had never seen before but my dad knew all about it. He stopped to talk to an old friend and we joined him for lunch. Mary and my little brother laid down to rest in the shade of a sycamore tree. Dad bought me some baklava made with honey and he let me have two pieces! Then he sent me to have a nap with my mother and little brother while he continued talking with his friend.

I saw the biggest donkey ever while in Jericho. It belonged to a lady called Rahab. The donkey was carrying two huge jugs and Dad said they contain red dye and rope. He said that after the rope had been in the dye for a time they would sell a piece of it to people who would go home and dye cloth with it. There was also a man who made reins for donkeys and leather sandals, a family weaving baskets, a wood-carver making spoons and bowls with covers, and a copper-smith making large bowls and trays.

In Jericho there was a lot going on all the time. There was music and dancing and people juggling fruit but the oddest thing I saw was a very tall man, his great height was obvious even from far away. It looked like he was 12 foot tall. I couldn't take my eyes off him as he got closer. When the crowd finally broke where I could see all of him I stood up but was disappointed as it was a man standing on another man's shoulders.

Later I saw a camel caravan which came through kicking up dust and I could barely see that there were riders on the camels in cages with curtains on them and Dad said they were from Ethiopia. The camels themselves had colorful braided ropes that matched the colors of the cages.

Just as we were leaving Jericho we stopped at a produce market and bought pumpkins, cucumbers, root vegetables, eggplant, and leeks. And now we had all we could handle. Boaz, our donkey, was heavily laden and Mary had to walk. Dad had my littlest brother strapped on his back as we headed for home. I told my dad that someday I want to go back to Jericho. I liked that place.

Draw your own picture below:

Six

We are home in Nazareth. The first night back I slept in the bed that my mom made for my brother and me. The bed-bag was freshly filled with hay and the wonderful smell helped me to sleep. We had new robes that Mother had made us before we left Egypt so we were very comfortable in the coolness of the night.

Early in the morning I looked out the window and saw the sun coming up. My Heavenly Father was at work. As I gazed around our yard I spotted my father's carpentry shop. The sign on the door said closed. Then I saw a stack of wood that had been drying all the time we were gone. Father had told me a lot about collecting wood and all the things you had look for and do with the wood before you could begin making things with it. He said he would teach me how to work with wood and he said "If you can think of it we can build it."

I heard Mom call us for the early morning meal. Some neighbors had brought us bread, goat's milk, cheese, and fresh pomegranate juice to drink. That was the start of my first day where I would spend my childhood years as a carpenter's son learning my father's trade. Our donkey Boaz, was waiting for his water, grain, and clover. He greeted me with his "heehaw" like he was happy to be home. Boaz was faithful to our entire family but if you were a stranger, would just give you a look that said "I don't listen to your instructions and I definitely am not moving for you."

My first baby sister was born in Nazareth. Mother Mary was so happy to have a girl. Father put up a new sign on the carpentry shop that said Joseph and Sons. He instructed me how to put the double baskets on Boaz and we went looking for more wood and firewood in the forest. Along the way we met many of our relatives. We stopped in Cana and ate the lunch Mom had packed us. Dad bought Mom some clay pots that she needed to store wine and olive oil.

We returned home at sunset and Mom and my brothers and sister met us at the front gate. We got together to give thanks for a beautiful day with water fresh from the well and talked excitedly about possible adventures for tomorrow. Boaz was waiting for his water and for us to take those heavy baskets off. Everyone worked together and Mom spotted her new clay pots. She did a little dance and gave Dad a kiss.

It was getting dark so we went inside. Dad lit the lamps and said he would show me how to make fire someday soon. The oven was still warm and we had fresh flat bread with herbs and cheese. Yum. Dad taught us a song from the scroll he had been given by a rabbi years ago. He sang to us and we sang with him and we learned Psalms 100:

"Make a joyful noise unto the Lord all ye lands, serve the Lord with Gladness. Come before His presence with singing. Know ye that the Lord is good. It is He that hath made us and not we ourselves. We are His people and the sheep of His pasture. Enter into His gates with thanksgiving and into His courts with praise. Be thankful unto Him and bless His name. For the Lord is good. His mercy is ever lasting and His truth endure to all generations."

Seven

The decision was made to go to the Sea of Galilee to get fish. Boaz had his double baskets and he was carrying many wooden buckets and several donkey yokes for plowing and one wooden chicken cage that Dad had made to barter for fish. It was a heavy load for Boaz but he didn't seem to mind and our family walked beside him except the new baby Mom carried.

Our first stop was the synagogue at Capernaum where we joined the rabbi and cantor. I always learned a lot from the scholars at synagogues. I learned how to read at a very young age. Every synagogue had scrolls and I was allowed to try to read one scroll at a time. It was like the Heavenly Father was speaking to me on a personal level and I began to know things in my heart and when I spoke to my mother about it she said "I know, for I have kept many things hidden in my heart."

Our friends Peter and some of his family, and future Mother-in-law lived in Capernaum. When we left the synagogue we went to visit them and stayed for a day. We got to visit the flour mill and watch the donkeys going round and round turning the mill stone on wheat to make flour. My mom bartered a wooden bucket for a bag of flour. Then we went to the winery and watched them dump a huge basket of grapes into a mechanical press and we watched the grape juice run out into clay jars. The wine maker gave each one of us a small taste of this sweet juice.

There were lots of adventures in Capernaum. I saw many interesting things and spotted a lizard going in circles. My brother James and I tried to catch it but it was faster.

They had black rocks in Capernaum and I picked up many and Mom helped me make a leather bag to put them in.

    We went to the Sea of Galilee the next day and Peter took us to a spot where there were many colors of smooth and beautiful stones. I found lots of white stones there. Peter's father explained to me that when they were going to take a judgement vote on someone, everyone was given a white stone and a black stone. If you were for the person you threw in a white stone and if you were against them you threw in a black stone. The stones were counted and those with more white stones were accepted and those with more black stones were rejected.

Peter taught us a game we could play with small objects like pebbles. We would take ten pebbles and place them in a large circle and we would pick one stone and throw it in the air and while it is in the air we would try to get as many pebbles as we could without dropping the one in the air. I have a special round stone I use for this game that is easy to catch and throw.

    We met Thomas, Didymus, and Nathanael from Cana, the sons of Zebedee, Jonas, James, and John that day. They would become good friends. The next day Peter said "Do you want to go fishing with me?" I jumped up and down and spun around and said "Yes!" Peter, my dad, and I gathered up the nets and carefully placed them in the boat. My dad lifted me into the boat and pushed us off into the deep. After we were towards the middle of the lake, Peter said "Let us stop here, this is one of my favorite places, there are lots of fish." Peter threw out the net and it went out in a huge circle and dropped into the water. Peter let it sink for a while then began pulling on rope cords that closed the net onto the fish. When we hauled the net back in it was so full of fish all three of us could barely pull it aboard. We did this three more times and all four times the net was full when we pulled it aboard.

Father and Peter began to talk about what to do with all these fish. As we neared the shore there were many people who saw us go out and were waiting to buy fish. They brought baskets and we filled them. Some paid in dinar but most bartered with us for things like dried fish, cheese, cloth, bread, leather, rope, sandals, pots, and baskets. Father and Peter were singing and dancing and could hardly wait to get back to Peter's Landing to clean the nets and his boat. Many people kept coming during our busy work to talk about news from Jerusalem.

The next day I tell Peter that I look forward to seeing him again and was thinking about all the things I had learned from Peter when we set off back home. Dad talked about how important the festival in Jerusalem was going to be then he turned to me and said "Son, I have been thinking, we are going to raise some sheep and you will be the shepherd. We must find many branches and sticks as long as you are tall to build a fence." We picked up wood as we came upon it on our way home.

The pretty stones I collected on this trip became my first and last collection. I carried these stones the entire trip. I learned the lesson about being black-rocked or as some call it, black-balled on this trip. I felt in my heart that many will reject *me* but I know I would always be accepted by my family and the Heavenly Father.

From the bank of The Sea of Galilee

Eight

    Orders for windows, doors, and stools, were waiting for us when we arrived home. We had gathered and prepared ample wood for all these projects. Dad taught me how to use all the tools and I helped prepare wood for stool legs. He taught me also how to use the drill to make holes in the wood but it was too hard yet to do by myself.

    After the legs were on a new stool, Dad had me use burlap that he had purchased in Joppa from a ship from a distant land in the seaport at Ashdod and he showed me how to weave a chair seat. I was very pleased that he had taught me such a useable skill. I took the stool in the house and showed it to Mom and said, "Dad said I could give this to you, it is my first weaving job." Mother Mary was delighted for the special gift. She sat on it and said "It is just right. All my friends will want one."

I ran back to the shop and told Dad how happy Mom was about the stool. He said "Indeed, let's make some more." I said "Yes Dad, Mom said all her friends will want one."

Dad said we needed to get ready to go to Joppa again. I asked "Dad, can I go to Joppa with you?" Dad said, "Yes son and you will meet many wise men from all over the world. They dock their ships at Ashdod and we will be able to barter with them and buy things with the money we made from the fish. We will get to see Simon the Tanner again. We can also go to the synagogue where there will be many wise men and scrolls that are different from the scrolls in the synagogue here."

We set off for Joppa on the Great Sea (the Mediterranean), just my dad and me. We stayed at Simon the Tanner's house and I didn't like the smell but we stayed there quite a while.

Simon the Tanner gave me a lesson in tanning leather and making sandals, harnesses, rope, clothes, saddles, bags, and packs. He showed me how to make leather string and then he showed me that weaving leather is like weaving chair seats.

Joseph knew that Jesus' heart and mind was open to learning many things from wise men, friends, and family and Joseph was astonished about the things Jesus was teaching others from scripture.

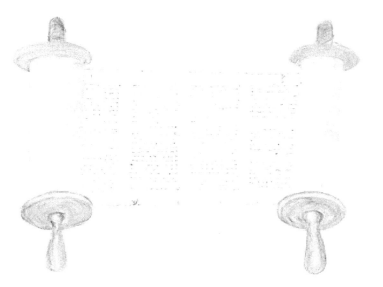

There was a knock at the door and Simon the Tanner opened it and there was Peter and many of his friends. They were invited in for tea that Simon had bought from a ship from a far-away land. I listened intently to all of their conversations. At times I would ask a question or make a comment and was treated with respect. I was talking about all sorts of things and they were listening intently. I spoke a lot about what the Torah and scriptures said and described what I learned from them about how people should live and what they should be waiting and watching for. Simon the Tanner spoke about how he made parchment for scrolls out of very thin untanned leather.

Leather Parchment

Nine

Mother Mary liked to have her own chickens; there is nothing like fresh eggs to boil and it was the girl's job to care for them. The girls had to bring water and while the chickens roamed freely during the day the girls brought them grain at night to get the chickens to come back to their coop for safety. They liked wheat grain best. Most of the chickens had names or a number and they became friends to the girls. Any time we felt hungry we could grab a boiled egg. They were a great meal to take on a day trip of play or adventure.

It was Friday and Mom was preparing the Sabbath food as no one worked during the Sabbath. She had sent the oldest sister to get a chicken for Dad to kill and prepare for plucking while the other girls watched. Now it was cooked and on Saturday afternoon, we sat for our main meal of the day. The girls started to cry as we were about to eat Number Seven. The girls would not take one bite of it. It was all the more for us boys. We all pretended to be sorry for the girl's great loss. They cried real tears and Mom could not console them.

***

I had a question, "Dad, when you took me to the temple to be circumcised was I really only eight days old?" He said, "Yes son, you are Jewish and all Jewish boys are circumcised on the eighth day." Jesus said "Did I cry for a long time?" "No son, the angel was there to take the pain away and that is the first time we called you Jesus. Your mother had been instructed while you were still in her womb that Jesus would be your name. I asked, "Dad do you know why God chose me to be his earthly son?" Dad responded, "You are just like all of your other brothers and sisters. However, your future is in the Heavenly Father's hands."

Jesus said, "Dad I really enjoy being a kid and having the joy of being a big brother and learning from all the elders in my life, like how I learned to be a servant to widows and the poor. The first time I brought a load of wood to the widow Martha my heart was filled with joy to see her eyes light up and to see how grateful she was. It was only a small task to me but meant a lot to her as it was far too heavy and too far to walk and she doesn't have a cart. I learn so much from them and my brothers and sisters like to learn from me and now we all enjoy helping others and they often ask to go with me and help someone in need."

Jesus relayed, "Dad you always answer my questions and you direct me to do good and make ourselves available even though sometimes we want to play. You let us help you build things and now, I believe, we have more hammer handles and stir sticks than anyone will ever need. We can give them as gifts!"

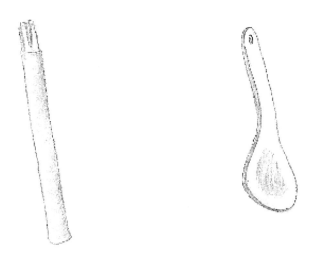

Joseph said, "Father God chose you for a very special task. In His time you will know it and you will truly be about your Heavenly Father's business, just like you are in my carpentry shop." Jesus said, "Dad I love to be with you on the Sabbath too. I learn so much as you teach from the scrolls. Going to temple with the whole family, eating a meal with friends and family, and the music and dancing is so rewarding. It lights up my insides and brings comfort and joy to my heart. It is like God the Father is working on my insides." "Yes son, when we keep the Father's commandments we have peace in our hearts. His joy renews our strength and menial tasks pass by quickly. "

Draw your own picture below:

Ten

Dad sent me to shepherd the sheep at a field far away where there was ample green growth. I love caring for the sheep. It wasn't a chore. When there I let my mind wander and always evaluated what I had learned on the Sabbath. One time there was a lion coming near and I brought all the sheep close to me and gathered stones to throw at that great big cat. The best part is that I actually didn't have to throw one stone. The cat looked at me eye to eye for a moment then turned and went back up the mountain. I believe my Heavenly Father protected us.

Jesus asked Joseph, who had stopped working and was staring out the window, "are you okay Father?" Joseph said, "I was thinking about how I brought you to Jerusalem to the temple as a baby and presented you to God the Father as the first-born boy, you were called holy to the Lord in more ways than one. I took an offering to the Lord on that day, a pair of turtle doves in a bird cage just like the cages I still build. I set them free during the offering. Simeon took you as an infant into his arms and he held you up to the Lord and prayed for you. He said something like this as he was praying for you in the temple "Now I have seen the Christ, I can face death." Wow, Dad, I want to meet Simeon. When can we go?

Joseph said he has gone on to heaven but we can visit his family when we are in Jerusalem. Joseph said, Jesus, I remember one more thing Simeon said when he was praying for you in the temple. He said, "For my eyes have seen thy salvation." Then Joseph said to Jesus "only God the Father can reveal to us what all Simeon said."

Son you have a heavenly understanding when you read the scrolls. When you read them or interpret them for your brothers and sisters and others, your insights are inspired, you have a gift.

The glory of the Lord is upon you and your mother and I like your way of blessing our family and friends. We are amazed at the things people are saying about you. The rabbi and the cantor say you even teach them. The Heavenly Father has told your mother many secrets that she keeps hidden in her heart about you. Maybe one day when you get much older she might share some details with you.

***

The family was invited to a vineyard at Kefr Kenna that is on the road to Capernaum. We were to pick grapes and fill the baskets on Boaz and our new donkey Barley. Mom would dry the grapes into raisins. We love her raisin cakes! Dad had brought Mother cinnamon from the ship at Ashdod on the big sea from an earlier trip. She used it sparingly but always put it in raisin cakes. It was Friday and preparations were being made for Sabbath, Mom made kosher cinnamon raisin cakes to take to the synagogue.

John, my brother and friend, was very bright, loving, and kind. We really stay together everywhere we go and sometimes went to synagogue together with Mother Mary and listened to her prayers. While at the synagogue we enjoyed being with the scholars of the day.

***

The Jewish girls and women always went to the synagogue on the Sabbath to worship the Heavenly Father. As they worship and pray, we listen and they pray for all the boys and girls for all of our needs, for the sick, and for miracles for the lost and the downtrodden. Dad decided we needed to go with him and be with the men from now on. They too prayed wonderful prayers.

The very first time I saw a six-pointed star was when John and I were at the Synagogue. Dad said he could make some out of wood to give as gifts. I thought of all the people in my life and how each one had made a difference. I thought that these stars might be a blessing for them. I think about my future and all my Heavenly Father has prepared for me. This star has meaning in it for Jewish people. The six-pointed star came from the line of King David and was the symbol of him that was on his shield.

***

There was a centurion who was one of my father's dearest friends. He was different from most of the other soldiers. They enjoyed each other's company and walked about talking about things he didn't understand and wanted to know.

Eleven

Dad told us boys we needed to gather more limbs, taller than we are, from trees that had fallen because we needed to build the fence higher because it was time to get goats. He said, Jesus your brothers can look after them but goats can be troublesome at times. They will get out of the pen so we must build it as high and as strong as possible.

The boys took Boaz and Barley and loaded them high with long limbs. By the time they got back to the house it was dark. Dad told the boys the goats are not like the sheep. Sheep will follow the shepherd but goats will go every direction that is why it will take all four of you boys to chase after them from time to time.

After we had the goats for some time, we knew where to look for them when they got loose. The goats liked to visit the widows and the kids and eat the wild flowers along the way. We had several does that had to be milked morning and night. This was a time when they were obedient and came home for Mom to milk them.

We all love fresh goat's milk and Mom made the best goat cheese and leben. We had trouble with our huge male goat Giant. Giant had a habit of butting the sheep, butting my little brother, butting Mom when she was milking the female goats, and making the girls run to get out of his way. Giant would climb on top of our flat roof where Mother had many herbs, fruit, and fish drying for winter to try and eat what he smelled up there. Dad blocked the stairs to the roof but that didn't stop Giant. Eventually, Dad had to make a heavy-duty door to close off those steps. Giant moped around for days until he noticed the neighbor's stairway was open and he helped himself to all the dried lizard skins and snake skins that their dad was going to take to Joppa to sell to Simon the Tanner. He didn't eat them he just broke them apart and kicked them off the roof. They were no longer worth anything and Dad had to make amends. For a week we had to search for and find lizards and snakes to make up for the ones Giant ruined. From that point on we put a bell around Giant's neck so we knew where he was going.

***

Living in Nazareth I really became strong in many ways. I was the tallest of all my brothers. Dad said he was watching me every day increasing in wisdom and the Grace of God was upon me. I was almost a man and was allowed to make a shepherd's sling for myself. Father taught me of the dangers of this weapon and told us the story of David and Goliath. My brothers wanted me to make them shepherd's slings just like mine and Father said I could but I must also teach responsibility and the dangers of using it in the wrong way. My brothers and I quickly became good marksmen. We used rotten stumps as targets. We put so many stones into one stump that it splintered into kindling.

I went to father's carpenter shop and asked if we could go to Jericho and Ein Gedi and swim in the Dead Sea. We have become so good with our shepherd's slings I believed we could feed the whole family with a small deer or several rabbits. The area around Ein Gedi had many wild animals. We could take Boaz, Barley, and our cart and fill them up with dates, figs, and food bought in Jericho and dried meat from the animals we were able to take with our slings. Joseph replied "Yes we will, someday. It would seem that we could do that on one of our trips to Jerusalem but it would add so much time to our trips. I am not comfortable putting that extended burden on our neighbors to look after our home and animals. Perhaps we should take a separate trip to those places one day. I will talk with your mother. I am sure the girls would enjoy the waterfalls at Ein Gedi."

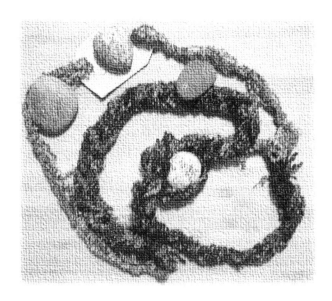

Two Slings

***

Mother Mary had a dear friend named Mrs. Dothan, who lived in Dothan and who had many children. It was in the land of Samaria where we would go for an unusual type of olive. We would even pick up those that had just dropped on the ground and they were very plentiful. These olives were larger than the ones from Nazareth. We kids made this job a fun adventure and tried to see who would fill their basket first. In the process the boys would try to grab a handful of olives from the girl's baskets and the girls would try to take the boy's olives.

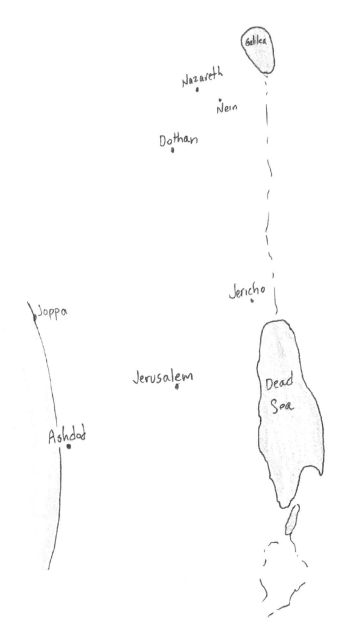

Map of the area with Ashdod on the Mediterranean

We also played a game among the trees where one kid would close their eyes and the rest of us would hide in the grasses, behind bushes, up trees, and behind large rocks. I was always last to be found. I could place my body on the back side of a tree and just move around as others looked for me. The Dothan kids called the game hide and seek. More and more children came to play. When it was my turn it was so much fun trying to find 20 kids. We played until everyone had a turn to be "it." Not everyone could count so the person that was "it" waited a fair amount of time before coming and looking for us.

Dad and Mr. Dothan roasted a goat and Mom had brought bread from her sand-oven. After dinner, Mr. Dothan said we have plenty of time to go to the olive press. When we arrived with our many baskets of olives, Benjamin, the olive-press man, was glad to see all the kids. He asked my dad, "is this your tribe?" Mr. Dothan stepped up and said "they are half mine."

Benjamin said "Kids let me give you a lesson on how to make the best olive oil. Each of you dump your olives in here, this is the press." Each of us dumped our olives in. Benjamin said his press the newest type of press for making the finest olive oil. He said it was better than using a mill stone, had less waste and spoilage and made a better quality oil. As Benjamin lowered the weights that were suspended above, by going hand over hand with a rope and pulley, the oil ran out and continued running out as many clay pots were filled with the first press of the olive oil.

Benjamin said, "Okay kids now I am going to show you how we are going to do the second press. You are going to be surprised. But before we do that here is a piece of bread for each of you." Benjamin scooped a cup of fresh olive oil and said "I want you all to taste this first press for the fine flavor and quality." Each kid dunked their bread. We all agreed it was very good.

Benjamin said "now watch." Benjamin took a big paddle that Dad had made for him and he stirred all the remaining smashed olives and pits to make them fit evenly under the press and he said to us "now I could add some more olives at this time but it would no longer would be first-pressed and the taste would no longer be the same."

Here goes the second press. Benjamin lowered the weights again hand over hand on the rope. He put the press up and down a few times and the oil flowed again in to a new jar. When it stopped flowing Benjamin said it was time to have another taste test and he scooped the cup into the new olive oil and we all tore off a piece of bread from a new loaf and dipped it in the new oil from the second press. As we smacked our lips we all agreed that it wasn't as tasty as the first press and definitely not as clear in color.

I asked, "Benjamin are you going to do a third press?" Benjamin said yes, we need to stir what is left real good first and push everything into the center. Benjamin lowered the press many times on the remaining pits and pieces that had been scraped from the corners and off the weights. A very small stream began to flow. And Benjamin again announced taste testing time. Another loaf was passed around and we all took a piece. We all dipped our bread in the third press oil except Benjamin and he stepped back and watched our reaction to the taste of the third press. Jokingly he said "nice right?" to all the yabuis (yucks) from the children. I said no that is not tasty at all. Benjamin said, "Can I tell you what the lesson is here?" All the kids said yes. Benjamin said "This is what your mother makes soap out of to keep you clean and your skin from drying out. It does wonders on your feet." The kids all say yabui and yuck again. Benjamin continued "It is also healing from exposure from the sun.

I have another lesson to teach you. The kids started to leave, Benjamin said "Okay here it is, you know those clay oil lamps you buy from the pottery shop? Do you know why they burn so long and give so much light? It is this third press oil that your parents use in every lamp." "Oh wait, I have one more story to tell you. You know these pits? Well we dry them out and your mother uses them to start the fires in her oven. They burn completely leaving no ashes and they make a good hot fire that smells good with very little smoke. Okay kids any questions?" "I have a question I said. You have oil on you from your shoulders to your toes and your arms are covered in it, does it ever all come off when you wash?" Benjamin answered "No, I am the best-oiled dad in all the land and it keeps me healthy."

When Jesus Turns Twelve

We returned to Nazareth from Joppa. Boaz and Barley climbed the hill to Nazareth where we stopped to buy fresh produce from a local seller. Joseph said "Son, it is time for you to study for your Bar Mitzvah. The family will be waiting for us and we can celebrate with all the things we have brought home from Joppa. Jesus said, "I am sure brother Simon will love his first belt and just think everyone gets a new pair of sandals. Mom will like all the spices we got from the ships. The barley we got from Galilee will be a blessing for Boaz and Barley." I asked, "Dad, do you remember when we got the new baby donkey and named her Barley? Joseph said, Yes I remember asking what you want to name her, and you said, "Let's call her Barley because she carried half of it back." And Barley it was.

***

Father, I was thinking about the cantor and all the scriptures he is going to be teaching me for the Bar Mitzvah. My Heavenly Father has already provided much information. The cantor will be surprised to learn how much I already know." Joseph said "There are five books in the Torah: Genesis, Exodus, Leviticus, Numbers, and Deuteronomy." Jesus replied, "Yes, the rabbi in

Jerusalem taught from the Torah and it was like I already had some of that information provided from the Heavenly Father so my understanding is better." "Yes son you will learn much from the cantor that will guide your life and you will have wisdom, knowledge, and understanding way beyond your years."

The day came for the celebration at the synagogue at Nazareth. The rabbi, many scholars, and all the local people gathered as twelve year old boys gathered around the cantor. Each boy was given a scroll to read from and to recite the verses they had learned. When it was his turn, Jesus stepped up to the podium and recited many verses from the Torah. The cantor looked at him deeply and said "You are a fine young man with a future that is in God the Father's hands." Joseph put his arms around Jesus and said "God the Father has trusted me to be your earthly father and you are a great blessing to us and to everyone who meets you."

***

It was the time of the Passover and all the relatives and friends took donkey carts in a caravan to Jerusalem. It was the custom to go to the feast there. It had been part of the family tradition for years. Many days were spent around and in the temple with rabbis and scholars. After about a week, the group of family and friends gathered on the temple steps to say goodbye to the rabbis and scholars and then the group started making their way back home to Nazareth.

After a day on the road, when Joseph and Mary and the kids got together for dinner, they realized Jesus wasn't with them. Joseph told his family to continue on home with the relatives and friends and Joseph and Mary went back to Jerusalem to find Jesus. They looked for three days in the market places, at friend's houses, the stables, and among the widows and poor and finally found him in the temple in the midst of teachers and scholars interpreting scrolls and speaking of the future. The scholars were rapt and looked astounded. Mary said to Jesus" I was worried!" Jesus said "Why did you spend all that time looking for me? Did you not know I would be about my Heavenly Father's business?" Joseph said "Come on son, pick up your bag, we are going home."

Draw your own picture below:

Thirteen

Now I am said to be a man, I will soon be thirteen. My dreams are full of portent. In my heart I seem to be getting more and more wisdom and understanding for who I will become. These gifts from the Heavenly Father are being made real to me and I feel refreshed and restored in my spirit, in my mind, and body.

Today I will work with my dad Joseph. As always, he teaches me many ways to build things with the wood we have gathered; there are many ways to make a basket. I also have many ideas about new inventions that would make carpentry easier and leather more helpful. Now I am building a large paddle to help take stuff from the large outside oven so we don't drop it in the dirt as often. It is Mother Mary's birthday and she will be surprised.

Father Joseph is making Mary a table one foot high and large enough for the whole family to sit around. This table will also be used when we have school. Today my brothers and I read from scrolls that came from Egypt.

My sisters are all busy with Mother Mary. They are learning how to weave cloth. My sisters began to make wool yarn from the sheep and then they began knitting winter clothes for us and blankets for the animals. The cooking smells of the lamb, vegetables, and baking bread caused our stomachs to protest the emptiness; we looked forward to the evening meal.

Yarn Spindle

***

Mother Mary and the girls went to the edge of the village and in a large tree they found a bee hive. They waited until nightfall and took the whole hive and put it in a cloth bag and a basket to contain all the bees. At home we let the bees out and they went off in a swarm to search for a new place to build another hive. We had so much honey we filled all of the small clay jars and we gave some to the neighbors. We also had more wax for candles. We took mutton fat and mixed it with wax from the beehive and made candles that gave off a wonderful smell and lasted a long time.

Honeycomb

***

Now that I am thirteen, Father trusts me to travel further from home. I always enjoyed being able to go fishing in Galilee and playing in the Jordan River. I heard the Heavenly Father tell me what Peter had said before "That I will be a fisher of men." I wasn't clear about what that meant.

On our next trip to Galilee we met Peter at his landing where he was mending nets with Peter's and Jesus' friends James and John. They said they would take us out in the boat and throw out a net and we could take the fish. We had Boaz and Barley and they both carried double baskets. I got to pick the spot to cast the net and it came up full of fish again and again. When we got to the shore we loaded the fish into the baskets to take home to Nazareth. Peter said, "Go to Tiberias on your way home and buy some salt." We went quickly up the hill to Nazareth. As soon as we arrived we went to the fish market and the owner of the fish market was ready to help us to clean the fish and preserve them with the salt we had bought. The owner sold the fish guts to a heathen woman to feed her pigs.

Jordan River

Fourteen

My family was going to Magdala for the feast for the opening of a new synagogue. A rabbi came from Jerusalem and met with the new elders to prepare the dedication and the kosher meal that we would all enjoy. We brought challah bread and garlic. Our neighbors and cousins that lived in Magdala had prepared vegetables and roasted meat. The wine came from Canaan, enough for everyone. The cantor and the rabbi began to sing and dance and the circle of dancers started out small but got so large it filled the street. I learned new dances with praises and worship at the same time.

I met Mary of Magdala for the first time, she was about the same age and she spent a lot of the time with our family and was a wonderful dancer. The musical instruments were played by young people and very old people alike. I like the string instruments and tambourines best. This service lasted well into the night.

We prepared our beds in the courtyard with many other people that came from a distance. This was truly a highlight in my life to be in Magdala for the new temple dedication, meeting new friends, and hearing new instruments. I may not be able to sing but I appreciate good music.

My father and I were sitting at the gate waiting for others. He said, "Jesus I wanted to talk to you about another lady in your life when you were a baby. Her name was Anna the daughter of Phaniel and she was from the tribe of Asher. You met her in the temple in Jerusalem last year. She was advanced in years, do you remember?" I replied, "yes." Joseph continued, "She lived with her husband for seventy years and had just recently become widowed. She was 84. When she met you, she told me that when she listened to you she became inspired and from that point she never left the temple, serving night and day and was often seen in prayer. She gave thanks for your words about the redemption of Jerusalem. She said, "Joseph I just prayed for the boy and gave thanks for all that God has planned for him."

Fifteen

There was a huge sycamore tree down by the road not far from our house. My brothers and I borrowed a coil of rope from Father's shop and a piece of branch that had been split in two so that one side was flat and about a foot long.

At the tree we picked the lowest and biggest branch and we hefted James up onto it so he could help us tie each end of the rope to the tree securely. The low point of the rope was about two feet off the ground and we tried to tie the "seat" on the rope but it kept falling off when we sat on it.

I didn't want to do anything permanent to the seat because I was sure Dad was going to use the wood for making something for someone. The girls had seen what we were doing from a window and soon all of us kids were out under the sycamore trying to figure out how to make it work.

I went back to the shop and got more rope and tied several loops around each end and securely fastened them. We undid the rope from the branch and tied the ends of the big rope to the loops of rope at each end of the seat. We then took the middle part of the big piece of rope further up the tree and wrapped it round and round a branch and tied it firmly so the seat was just the right height off the ground.

    We sat the youngest of us on the seat and gently pushed and the swing worked perfectly. We were all clapping and laughing. I pushed all of my sisters and brothers and they had several turns each. I felt something and turned and saw Mother and Father by the house, hand in hand, watching us with smiles on their faces.

Draw your own picture below:

Sixteen

Dad often gave us time to play and we were creative about thinking of new ways to have fun. One day Father had finished making many wheels of all sizes and he was checking to see if they rolled correctly. We said we would help and we boys rolled them back and forth across the yard, pushing harder and harder, trying to roll them too fast for the others to catch. We found that we could roll them faster by pushing with a stick and getting a running start and we rolled the wheels across the yard and down the street and laughed at each other running to try and catch them. We could make a game out of almost anything. Father said "From now on it is your job to verify the wheels are balanced."

Jesus, as your earthly father, you brought me much delight and joy. Your mother and I have shared many times with each other about how you have made great choices to care for others and you have learned so much from the scrolls of knowledge and the Torah and many other books that I have heard you use to pray for yourself and others. God the Father has heard your every prayer. He has gifted your future with miracles.

Joseph said, "Jesus do you remember that Passover when you were just twelve years old and you had a lot of growing to do?" Jesus said "Yes and these have been great years of discovery. Dad, I am sorry I did not tell you I was staying behind when the caravan left Jerusalem when I was twelve, I was still hungry for spiritual things." Joseph replied "I hope you learned a good lesson from all the anxiety you caused me and your mother. You had always been such an obedient boy that it was a shock to learn you stayed without telling us." "I am sorry Father that was irresponsible of me. I did learn the lesson. Never has it been so clear that everything we do affects others now and into the future." Joseph said "Jesus you have been a delight to me, your mother, and all our family and friends who know you well. We love you deeply."

Father, I still have a lot to learn. We encounter people from time to time that are just mean. Like the pig lady who bought the fish guts. I have been kind each time I have seen her and she still puts her stick out as if to hit me even when I tried to give her a small gift or ask how she is doing. In our travels I have seen many people that were not easy to be next to. Why do I feel uncomfortable around them? Joseph said, "You have the gift of discernment. Not everyone knows who to keep away from and it affects their life negatively for a long time. It is a gift from the Heavenly Father to be aware of who we can befriend."

Draw your own picture below:

Seventeen

On one cold winter day Dad surprised us with a new cart. We had seen it being built but had no idea it was for us. Dad said it was made just for us boys to use as we help widows, orphans, and the needy in the village. "They need fresh water from Nazareth and the cart will help you bring enough." The widows especially needed help because they were getting too old to gather firewood and haul stuff to and from market. A widow would walk with us and the cart to the market to buy fish, flour, honey, salt, and oil for food and lamps. Our cart could help many at one time and we often made a group outing of it.

Anyone in need knew we had the cart and often someone would come get us to help someone else. We boys just seemed to have it in our hearts to serve the widows and others in need. Many young widows still had children and we would bring robes that my mother and sisters made, sandals, and treats from our home to theirs. It was always a great blessing for us to be able to give to others and Dad often did repairs for them. One time we helped Dad repair our neighbor's roof in the rain by adding new tiles over a hole.

When we went to Simon the Tanner's he always brought out the new sandals for all the orphans. Dad taught us to make ourselves available to be good helpers where ever we saw a need. One time we saw a widow's goat in a field far from her home. We made a harness out of weeds and took off running for it and so did the goat in the opposite direction. We spent most of the day trying to catch that goat and laughing. When we finally delivered it back to the widow she was very thankful as it was just in time for milking.

We boys all learned how to build fires and because of our many trips with Dad we learned to cook fresh fish over the fire. Mom liked it when we cooked fish outside because it took extra wood to burn the fish smell out of the inside oven. Mom would always ask, "Boys do you want your bread and soup to smell like fish?"

Dad made a new sand-oven with a clay pot lid for Mom so she could make ample bread for us and have some left to sell at the market each week. All the ladies get a day off from baking their Sabbath bread when our cart takes the bread Mom makes to the market.

Preparing the food for the Sabbath makes our Fridays busy preparing meals but we all help and that makes it fun. We will soon be going to Capernaum for more flour, wheat, barley, and oats. We can carry more in the cart than we could have on Boaz and Barley alone.

***

Brother Simon said "Jesus, we always get excited when you build a fire and say you are going to cook the family meal because I have been waiting a long time!" The family laughed and Jesus said "Well today is the day and Mother gets a break." Mom and the rest of us sang and danced in glorious expectation.

I made the dough and let it rise then placed the garlic on a rock next to the fire and worked the dough into small loaves by rolling pieces in a ball and then flattening it out by smacking my hands together. I put the dough in the hot sand-oven. When the garlic was done I rubbed the soft garlic paste and salt on the fish and placed them on the hot rocks. I lifted the ceramic lid off the oven and when picking up a loaf I noticed all the loaves were stuck to each other because I put them too close together. I tried to pull one from another and they all fell in the ash. My first reaction was to reach in and pull them out. We got ash bread for dinner and I got burnt fingers.

The widow ladies and orphans had been invited at our table this day to enjoy the tasty food and one of the widows suggested putting honey on the ashcakes. After everyone was sure I wasn't too badly hurt we laughed. A lot! I had to keep putting my hand in a pot of water to soothe the burns. In all the laughter a widow laughed out "This was so fun Jesus, when are you cooking again?" The pained look on my face with my hand in the water suggested it would be a very long time.

Draw your own picture below:

Eighteen

Jesus told a story as a testimony at the temple in front of the people. He had gone to Jerusalem alone. He said his life had been truly blessed by his great earthly family. "We have grown together spiritually. We love each other and accept each other. We walked through this land with one heart caring for one another and I and my brothers and sisters grew up doing all the things that children do but we were never malicious. We were always for each other's best interest. I must say our lives have been an adventure as we held each other's hand, danced and sang of the Lord with the high praises of God on our lips, with thanksgiving always for the great God that we serve as we celebrated each day."

***

Joseph said "Jesus what are you thinking?" Jesus talked about how each year the family goes to Jerusalem for the festival. "We hear so much about the dates and figs from Jericho and many elders have told me the stories of Ein Gedi. I heard about the waterfall that is in front of the cave where King Saul hid from David." Joseph replied oh my, yes son that is true. Jesus said, "I have read the scrolls and heard stories about Jericho. It is also told that the Dead Sea is a great place to go and soak your feet. Its waters are healing, and I heard that you can float on top of the water without sinking. I don't know if I believe it but I would like to go. Do you remember me asking years ago?" Joseph said, "I remember, yes son we will make plans for the whole family to go. I am sure you will get a deer with that shepherd's sling."

We could talk about nothing but the city of Jericho, Ein Gedi, and the Dead Sea. Joseph reminded us we would go by way of the road next to the Jordan River. He said we would see lots of Roman soldiers because they had a fortress a few miles away at Masada. We could all fish and swim. All I can say about this right now is that while preparing to go, there was joy with singing and dancing among all my family. We had waited a long time.

We prepared our supplies for the wonderful family trip and my brothers and I practiced using our shepherd's slings. The days passed so slowly and the night before leaving we could hardly sleep. Off we went down the path to the road that leads us to our destination. Barley and Boaz looked like they were dancing and kicking up dust as they trotted alongside the family.

Along the way there was so much to see and much to talk and sing about and be thankful for. We are some of God's chosen and we are grateful. We boys were dancing along the road with our sisters, we too were kicking up dust. Father and Mother were coming behind hand in hand praising the Lord with all He had provided. I heard Mom say over and over, how blessed she was for all of us kids. They were praising the Lord for each other and for the plans God had in mind for each of us. We met many of our distant relatives, friends, and strangers on the way there and many said they had never been to Jericho or Ein Gedi and wanted us to stop on our way back to let them know how it was.

A big blessing was about to happen as the day was ending and a new day was coming with lots of adventure. Oh, how we boys loved adventure. We met a caravan from Egypt on its way to Jerusalem. Dad bartered with them and gave them a wooden bucket, a stir stick and a hammer handle for a bag of corn.

We had wonderful meals with corn the rest of the way and Dad saved seed to plant at home in Nazareth.

The next day as we were almost to Ein Gedi, a shepherd with a flock of sheep stopped to visit and Dad bought a sheep and fresh cheese in exchange for a bird cage, a bucket, a hammer handle and a stir stick.

The shepherd had been to Ein Gedi many times and told us about the water-well that was there and how to climb the rocks to the cave behind the waterfalls. We were getting really excited. The next day we stopped at the Dead Sea. This was a big adventure. The water was so salty and hot it burned our mouths. We found out it was true, you could float on the top without sinking.

The Dead Sea

We left the Dead Sea and hurried to Ein Gedi for fresh water to wash all that salt off. We laughed and splashed each other from the well water and poured cool water over the girls. Barley and Boaz were hee-hawing as they smelled the sweet water and Dad gave them each their own bucket of water. They drank the buckets dry and laid under the sycamore trees to sleep. The girls went to the forest and picked grass and flowers for Boaz and Barley to eat and to put flowers in their hair. We all drank a lot of this sweet cold water. It was so good, and we filled up every container.

We boys ran up the mountain side with our shepherd's slings not only for protection, but we had in mind to get an animal for dinner. Mother Mary built a fire while we hunted. A few hours later I came back with a small wild goat around my neck that we had already gutted and bled, and Mother roasted it for dinner for the family and dried the remaining meat for the next few days. Brother John prepared the skin for Simon the Tanner for later. Everyone enjoyed the meal under the stars.

Nineteen

I was very aware of people I could help, the blind, the thirsty, the naked, the lost, the sick, the hungry, prisoners, demon possessed, and our neighbors. One day a man walked into our village. He had obviously come a long way. Not only did he look worn but his clothes were thread bare and he had no sandals and only a beat up water-bag that had twine wound around several places to stop leaks. This was the extent of his possessions. I went to him and introduced myself. I gave him my lunch and shared my water. When I looked into his eyes I saw a man that was very broken and I asked if he would tell his story.

He said "Yes. I come from Jordan where I had a family and lived in a village not too different from Ammon. Everyone in the village got sick. We thought it was the water from the well so we began carrying water from the river but one by one people started to die. The first to go in my family was my youngest daughter Phoebe. As people continued to die they began to look to the animals as the cause. They did find one camel that had wandered into the village from somewhere they did not know. Upon examining this camel, they found foam in its mouth and his belly was full of sores. The elders of the village gathered together to kill the animal and burn it's carcass and then bury the ash remnants far in the mountains. After this was done many of the elders died within days. Then their wives and their children died.

My dear wife and all our children died. I sent for a rabbi from Jerusalem to pray for us. When he heard of the sickness in the village he refused to come. Within the next few months everyone in the village had died and I was alone. Because of my grief I just started walking. I don't know how long I have been walking but when I got here I felt I could go no further. My body is weak and worn. My sandals wore out a week ago. I have had very little to eat and very little fresh water.

Jesus said, "I have a pair of sandals in the shop I want to give to you. I am sure my father has an extra robe. Would you accept these gifts?" He answered "Yes, I do have a distant relative in Cana along this road." Jesus said, "Well, you don't have far to go it is just four miles. So, come home with me and refresh yourself and sup with us." He said thank you. Jesus asked, "What do I call you?" He said, "My name is Elias."

After cleaning up and in new clothes and sandals, Jesus and Elias entered the house and the family set out a large tray of foods and tea. Jesus introduced Elias and when you looked into his eyes you could see that a peace came upon him.

While eating and talking with the family, Brother Simon said he had just made a new water bag out of goat skin and he asked Elias if he could give it to him as Elias' bag was cracked and leaking. Elias took it with a grateful heart. Elias said to Simon, I am a potter and will be living close in Cana. I want to make you a wedding jug. Simon laughed and said "no hurry."

***

John (John the Baptist), my cousin from En Karen had come with his mother Elizabeth to visit my mother Mary (her sister), and the new baby. John told us about the elder men in Qumran who were called Essenes who cared for and transcribed the scrolls (what are known today as the Dead Sea Scrolls). John said to Jesus "Let's plan a journey for a special time of learning from the Essenes." They spoke to Joseph and Mary who agreed. John and Jesus packed their travel bags and, with Barley who carried provisions, camping gear, and gifts for the Essenes, set off. Jesus took his shepherd's sling to acquire meat along the way and intended to bring the animal skins to Simon the Tanner when they travelled through Joppa.

When they arrived at the Essene village they were shocked. There were no women or children anywhere. They were invited inside and saw lots of older men transcribing scrolls onto papyrus and parchment made from local sheep's leather.

Jesus was excited about learning and couldn't stop reading scrolls. John had to forcibly take Jesus to meals and bed; Jesus became so absorbed in everything he read. Jesus explained many of the insights he had since coming to this village with John, he felt this information was preparing him for the unknown that lay ahead. The hours and the days passed by quickly. Suddenly, Jesus realized it had been a month and told John he must return home. John said, "I will stay a bit longer, please let my mother know."

Twenty

Jesus and his family were at Ein Gedi. Ein Gedi has become an enjoyable yearly adventure. Jesus' brothers did not want to leave it was so beautiful; the girls and Mary so enjoyed the waterfalls. It was in front of the cave where Saul hid from David. There were many fruit trees around the waterfalls and the girls and Mother filled the donkey's baskets with dates, figs, apricots, herbs, and pomegranates. There was one thing about the trip that year that we never speak of, my brother's and I.

After gutting a deer we removed our clothes and washed them then hung them in the trees. We went in the water and stood under the waterfalls, splashed around, going under the water, standing under the force of the falls, and then standing behind the falls. While we were in the water talking we heard someone coming so we walked back behind the waterfall and waited awhile and when we came out everything was quiet. We looked at the tree where we had hung our clothes and we could see they were not there. We rushed out and when we got to the tree we saw our clothes were now on the ground beneath where they had been hanging. We picked up our clothes and quickly put them on and began to laugh. We thought we were going to have to go back into camp naked! We laughed so hard that we fell to the ground. We assumed our sisters played the trick, but we weren't going to give them satisfaction by mentioning it.

On the way home, we stopped at Simon the Tanner's and left our animal skins and had great fellowship while we were there. Simon presented the boys with blank leather scrolls and Dad said we could go to Ashdod to get ink. We are always thankful to Simon.

A rabbi dropped in with news from Jerusalem and read us a new scroll. It was from the book of Isaiah, chapter four, and we discussed it in detail and referred to Zachariah and Jerimiah and we discussed eternal life from the scroll of Joel that we had discussed earlier. The scroll really taught us about how we were to live and about the sin that needed to be washed away from our lives. Jesus relayed that verse five ensures that God will protect us.

***

I really enjoyed being at the city gate at every city we visited. Father Joseph had friends who he met at the city gates every place we visited and talked about what was happening in Jerusalem. We discussed scrolls that rabbis would bring, including those which were read at

Qumran, and my brothers took notes on their new leather scrolls.

We also discussed the garrisons of Roman soldiers that were new to the area including what information strangers brought from distant lands. Many were from Egypt, Ethiopia, and Moab off the Kings Highway. The Ethiopians brought many stories about the Arc of the Covenant. Somehow, I just knew in my inner most being that there would be a time I would need all this information, so my attention never wavered.

However, all this information from afar did put a desire in my brothers and friends to visit the many places the elders and travelers spoke about. We met people that came to the gate every day just to keep updated with news from Jerusalem. We became friends and we enjoyed sharing foods and tea. They all had many questions for the elders. It was very sad when we had to leave for home. I have been so blessed to have many friends that liked to learn and liked the things I liked. I kept old friends close and met new friends on my travels and adventures with my family and friends. I often thought about the next place we would sit at the gates and how we would explore ideas with others.

Twenty-one

John, my cousin, and I spent time together in En Karen with my aunt Elizabeth. She would go with us to the hillside to pick plants and berries that were in vast supply in the spring of the year. We learned to find the best berry bushes and always left a few berries on each plant to ensure next years continued growth.

I loved to eat berries while we picked them. By the end of the day my hands and lips would be purple. The little flat plants called Za'atar we pulled up and at home tied them in little bunches and hung them along a lengthy stick we found in the forest. Then we would tie the stick to the top of the widows outside to get lots of sun and air so the plants would dry out fast. From those plants Aunt Elizabeth added sesame seeds from her garden and other herbs. She made the best Zata. She had fresh olive oil and yogurt for us to dip our fresh loaf in and then adding Zata. I will never forget how delicious it was. The next time I went to visit my cousin John, we picked a ton of Za'atar to take home to the family so Mother Mary could make Zata for all of us to enjoy.

***

Brother John reminded us that we laughed till we cried when Jesus lifted a harp to try to make music. Not one note was clear, clean, or beautiful. His music sounded like Barley when she had her first colt. We all have been gifted but Jesus lost out on the gift of music. All he had to do was start singing or plucking the harp and we would laugh so hard and roll on the ground. But we always sang with him anyway.

The cantor was aware of our fun and took us boys aside and shared how much more Jesus had been gifted in other ways and that we should enjoy his gifts as he had taught us all to write, count, and to be servants to others. Most of all he shared the Heavenly Father with us in detail that we could apply to daily life.

Twenty-two

I was just back from visiting friends in Galilee and the day was very hot. We had been busy all day filling every pot with water per Dad's wishes. We hauled the big jars in our cart to be stored in case of a sandstorm. Dad had told us of sandstorms that last for days. Dad kept watching the sky and remarking how strange it was and different from normal summer days. Mary was busy with the sand-oven out by the door and she made more bread in one day than ever before. The air around the house was weirdly quiet. Not even the birds were singing.

After all the work was done my brothers and sisters asked Mom if we could eat some hot loaves. Mary said, "Yes my dear children and it will be delicious with honey and fresh goat yogurt." Mom called when it was ready, and we sat down at the table and started by giving thanks to the Most-High God for all His gifts and provisions. We bowed our heads and listened to what Mom said to God. She was always so thankful, and she had a thoughtful and grateful heart and a deep love for all of us in the family. After we ate, Mom had us take some fresh bread, honey, and fresh water to Dad in the shop. He hadn't come in for the meal because he was finishing orders as quickly as he could before the storm came.

Late in the afternoon Dad told us to look toward the west and pointed out the dark brown sky. He said "That is sand coming!" He also told us the wind is so strong it will blow you off your feet. Dad and the older boys hurriedly brought the chickens, the donkeys, the goats, and sheep to the barn room for safety. One of the hens had just had chicks hatch and had ten baby chicks under her wings. It was more than a handful to carry them all with the mother hen and Mom said we can bring them into the house so they don't get trampled. It wasn't long before we were all holding a chick. The girls named all the chickens and we had a good time laughing at the names they gave them. Some of them got numbers instead of names. We would pick one up, look it in the face and ask "Which one are you?" There was so much laughter.

The wind outside began to pick up and we could hear things being blown around in the gusts. The sound of the wind became *so* strong we could no longer hear each other talk and the sand began to come in around the windows and under the door. Father said we must cover the cracks with our robes to keep sand out and we also put wet cloths over the windows to catch more sand. In the middle of this roar of sand it got so hard to breathe that we also put cloths over our mouths. Mother said, "I would like to save some of that clean sand to wash the pots." Dad said, "You will have ample sand to save." He told us a story, "I was in one of these storms when I was a boy and the sand will be several feet high in places." About that time, we heard a crash of a tree falling and then another. Dad said it sounds like the trees down the hill. We didn't sleep much that night and we stayed together in the main room and told stories.

In the early morning everything got very quiet. Dad pushed open the door, pushing a foot of sand away and we all stepped out to look at the mounds and mounds of sand everywhere. We saw sand piled up high on the west sides of all the buildings in the village, sand covered the trees that fell, and left all the bushes looking like brown bumps. We could no longer see the ruts in the road.

Many people came out and joined us to talk about the storm and how hard it was to breathe or see. One of our neighbors said he was walking home from Cana and told us the story. He said, "The wind and sand made it so difficult to walk and I could not see. I hunkered down next to the road behind a tree, turned away from the blasting sand and covered myself with my robe and waited out the storm. I was fearful, but I prayed throughout for God to see me safely home. I am concerned about my family and animals, so I have to check on them now. I prayed to God to look out for all of us. We stood together listening to sand stories from others.

Walking back toward the house, Joseph said "Let's keep the animals inside the barn for a while more. I don't think we should let them out yet. All at once it got very quiet again. Father looked up at the sky and he said this is also just like it was when I was a kid. We are now going to have a rain storm. All at once the biggest drops of rain I ever saw began to fall. Buckets of water were falling from the sky. We couldn't safely look up. The streams of water began to run down the road in rivulets. We were immediately drenched and without a word we all took off running for our homes. I called it a sweet rain as it would wash everything clean.

After the rain subsided we went outside and repaired the fencing. The donkeys were making their noises loudly and wanted out of the barn but we had work to do. After we fixed what we could we opened the barn door and the animals began to pour out. The donkeys were heehawing, the sheep and goats were yelling "bah bah" and chickens all made happy clucky sounds in songs of praise as the animals rushed out of the confines of the barn.

Father went down to the city gate to hear the latest news on the sandstorm. The boys and I filled our cart with the extra water and bread to care for the widows and orphans. Many of the elders related sandstorm stories from long ago. One of Dad's customer said "Joseph, you will need to build many more shutters for our windows and make them sand proof this time." Joseph said "Sure and we need some glassmakers in town to use up all the sand we have." Everyone laughed. "When I go to Joppa I will get some Roman glass. My boys and I will go to Ashdod on the big sea to find material to build metal hinges, so the shutters close tighter to the windows. I am sure we can make flat wooden shovels that we can barter with at the port as they will need many to clear sand out of the city."

The wind in the forest blew down many trees and branches and blew a lot of bark off the trees. This saved us from having to remove the bark. My brothers and I went out with Boaz and Barley and we gathered wood and loaded them high. When we got back to the carpentry shop and unloaded, Dad was so pleased he began to dance and sing a new song.

These are my boys they bring me joy and delight. Oh, how they bring delight to Mother and me. My boys are the protectors of many sisters. They are gentle and grow into fine young men with respect for all. They are the sunshine in my life. They are always ready to serve with helping hands. Wise beyond their years with wisdom to share. My boys are creative adventuresome boys and are my gift from God above.

Still dancing and singing he said "Boys you can teach Boaz and Barley to haul even more wood by harnessing the ends of two long limbs to them and we could put small wheels on the other ends behind and using lacing and cross branches to make a bed. You could load so much wood on the carrier you could probably bring back a whole tree in one trip. There were many trees that had fallen in the storm. We will need to take a saw, axe, and rope or straps. They gathered what they needed and set off to get more wood and made many trips for several days.

Axe, saw, sickle, and wooden mallet

Twenty-three

The home town of Andrew was Bethsaida and was about an hour walk from Nazareth. Andrew is a fisherman along with Peter (the son of Peter the fisherman) and Phillip who all lived in Bethsaida. Andrew's home was on the Jordan River where it flows into the Sea of Galilee, not far from Capernaum. Jesus and his brother John were friends with Andrew, Peter, and Phillip. John, Andrew, Peter, and Phillip believed that Jesus was somehow different than they were. They had a strong connection with Jesus and enjoyed being in his company. Many times John, Andrew, Peter, and Phillip took trips together with Jesus to get updates from the cantor and rabbi knowing that many things were happening because of Jesus.

The synagogue at Bethsaida was made of white limestone and was very beautiful. The floor has mosaic tiles with pictures of birds, fish, flowers, and other animals. I reflected on the stories we learned at the synagogue as we sat with the elders at the gate of the city on our way home. One of the scholars in Bethsaida told us stories about the Canaanites, the Philistines, the Maccabeans, the Nabataeans, and of course Herod the

Great. It seems they all came and left something behind: buildings and altars to their gods.

We learned about another city called Bethsaida close by. We were told many stories about the people at the other town who sold dried fish. Many travelers came from all over to buy fish from that town and to barter. No one is sure why there are two towns so close with the same name but some say it was an ancient flood that split them in two.

Jesus had to leave to work in the harvest at home. The barley was ready early so a lot of activity was happening in every home and so many things from the garden needed to be brought home. All the kids were helping. Mother Mary had set up many racks made out of poles for drying. Harvest time was a beautiful time of the year and Dad said that this year we will have plenty for winter.

Harvest Vegetables

Starting to fill basket with threshed barley

***

I am one of Jesus' sisters and he is so faithful to all of us here in our home in Nazareth. In all of our adventures he always thought ahead to prepare a safe way for us. On these journeys he never walked by a stranger.

Jesus always brought hope to our family during difficult times and somehow was able to bring hope to others. Widows and orphans felt hope from the kindness and help they received from him. Even the sick, broken, and displaced were lifted back into the community by way of Jesus' acceptance and aid.

I remember one time our goat Giant came after Jesus. He stood up put his hands out and took hold of Giant's horns and pushed back with all he had. Giant let him push him back and Jesus ended up on the ground spread out like butter. While Giant stood there waiting for Jesus to get to his feet, Jesus looked at Giant and said "Come here goat, you have a twig in your ear. I will fix it for you." Old Giant walked up to Jesus and tilted his ear and let Jesus pull out the twig. Jesus had a special connection to animals.

Draw your own picture below:

Twenty-four

It was a very cold winter and we all gathered in the house around the oven to get warm. The water had frozen for the animals and the chickens. We boys told the girls "no worry we will care for your chickens today." Mom and the girls were preparing lots of food and bread to share with the widows and orphans.

One of Dad's friends said that Mt. Hermon had more snow this year than ever before. I told Dad I wished we had a horse. I would ride up there and see for myself. Dad said that would be nice, but it is just too far, better to go in the spring or summer. We could pack up Boaz and Barley and take the family on a big adventure.

Winter was long, and we were looking forward to spring. We spent many days planning how we would plant the garden in the spring with all the seeds we had stored in seed jars. We also talked about all the repairs we had to do after the long hard winter. We could already tell the goat's fence needed a lot of repairing. We could tell the animals were anxious for spring too because they were getting very restless.

When spring finally came it was so nice to have the sun warming us as we set out to do repairs and care for the animals. The chickens were clucking and having fun scratching in the mud. The sheep were baaing and the goats were jumping over each other. Mother Mary was happy to have a nice supply of fresh eggs once again and the girls were anticipating new chicks.

Draw your own picture below:

Twenty-five

We were talking about a previous visit to Bethlehem and that we are all related to David who was the king. Dad said David was a shepherd like I was. Dad had taken me to the cave and manger where I laid as an infant. The younger girls chimed in and said "what?" Yes, I laid in a manger where animals were sleeping. Dad then took us to Egypt because an angel told Dad we had to leave.

Did I tell you about how narrow the road to Bethlehem was Dad asked? Some places were barely more than an animal trail. There was barely room to pass anyone on the road and we were always worrying about meeting big groups like soldiers.

Jesus takes a turn and says "The rolling hills were just right for all the grazing animals. I rode my first horse in Bethlehem. It seemed like I was so high up. I really like horse saddles, and how they fit. I was not fearful of falling. The horse seemed to like me. Dad's uncle said I would make a good horseman. All the brothers wanted a ride so we went to a street with steps and turned the horse around so the boys could jump on. I lead them up the narrow streets then turned back to pick up another.

I talked about my desire to have a horse for the family and Dad said a horse eats more than Boaz, Barley and their children combined and doesn't do as much work. When you have a home of your own you can get a horse.

Draw your own picture below:

Twenty-six

Many people and places are in my mind and heart today. I feel so loved by my Heavenly Father and my earthly family. At this moment in my life, in my mind's eye I can see our family home in Nazareth where I am truly loved so deeply by my family. Mom always has my best interest at heart. She cares for me and the others so well, she prepares the very best food every day and Dad provides for our every need. He makes our home the place where we all want to be.

I remember my first bed-bag with the fresh hay Dad and Mom had prepared for me and my little brother when we got back from Egypt. The years passed quickly and I think back to each bed-bag that was prepared and how I always got the new ones as I was biggest and my sisters and brothers always had hand-me downs. Mother became a pro at making them as comfortable as possible by adding wool to the fresh hay and herbs. I will miss that comfort when I leave home.

***

The cart Dad had made for us was always ready to help someone out. Once we put an old man in the cart who had broken his foot in the olive grove. We took him to his home to be cared for by his wife and children. They wanted to pay us a day's wages with shekels and oil. We said no thanks, we are well cared for and are doing this because it is right and because we care. They insisted we stay for a meal, so we stayed and had fun with their family eating some of the jam the mother and daughters had made the day before. It was very tasty. We became good friends with the family and every time they saw us would ask if we had carried anyone else in our cart.

***

I remember the time Boaz and Barley had their first baby donkey. What an experience. Mother had more answers for us than Dad did. After that night of suspense waiting for Barley to give birth we heard the first cry and Dad came back and said, "it's a donkey." We laughed and then he said, "it's a boy." It reminded us of all the times we waited for him to come out and let us know when Mom had a new child.

Twenty-seven

The big accident. On the Way home from Canaan Dad had the biggest clay pot of special wine for the extended family who was coming from Bethlehem for Purim festival. We boys wanted to place it in the basket and let Barley take it. Dad said no, "I have a harness made for this purpose and I will carry it on my back more safely than the donkeys."

We were walking down the path towards home when Dad stepped in a rut and tripped. He hit the ground hard and the pot broke in pieces and Dad had a bath in the special wine. We all stopped and looked and saw that he was okay and then the laughter started. We laughed so hard we cried. Joseph said, okay from now on I am not a beast of burden and I will never again take a job from Boaz or Barley. This invention is a failure. He got to his feet, shook off some wine and danced down the road in his brightly stained robe and smelling like he had much too much wine to drink.

As we continued the walk home, when we passed others, they would look at Dad and would smell the wine and they would shake their heads and we would break out in laughter each time.

Twenty-eight

Our donkeys were the best entertainment, they could make you laugh. Barley was the creative one, she could unhook the gate to let the goats out for her little donkeys to play with in the yard and then would look innocent and let us blame the goats for getting out. The donkeys and the goats found lots of things to kick, climb on, eat and play with like the clothes drying on a rack or helping themselves to the barrel of apples by the front door. Mom would chase after them and they would go in every direction until she could catch a piece of the cloth they were playing with. The cloth would have goat teeth marks and footprints. This happened many times and the goats and donkeys loved the mayhem. There were times when we all joined the donkeys and goats on the run.

Twenty-nine

We had only been home a few days when Joseph became ill. He stayed in the house and Mother Mary cared for him. Some elders came and prayed for him. The Rabbi came and brought comfort by reading the scroll from Isaiah 40. I went to the shop and got caught up with all the orders. My brothers went up north with the cart and returned with ample wood for future orders. I so liked working in the shop with Dad that it feels lonely by myself. I asked my brothers and sisters to join me in the shop to cast out the loneliness.

Mother came and said "Come, you must come now." When we arrived it was moments later that the Heavenly Father took Dad. I felt like my heart would break, especially for my mom and sisters and brothers and close friends. All the women from the village dressed in black with their heads covered. They brought Mom a black robe and head covering. I will never forget the sounds the women make as they prepare a body for burial. It is a type of ululating sound that they made the whole day and night and at the tomb. That was a moment in time that I really felt like I was the man of the family. Dad had taught me well. I was more than ready to carry on with filling orders at the carpentry shop. My dear

Mother had become a widow with orphans. The great loss of her best friend and husband for twenty-nine years was much to bear.

Jesus said "They both gave me a good childhood, loving care, and the gift of many brothers and sisters to grow up with. One of the hardest days people remember is the day we say goodbye to our loved ones.

The latest news about Jesus and all the things and miracles that were taking place in Galilee was spreading to the friends and relatives in Bethlehem, Jericho, Joppa, Capernaum, Magdala, and many of the local people who watched Jesus and his brothers and sisters growing up knew Jesus was the oldest son of the carpenter in Nazareth. Many strangers and customers who came to order and pick up the finished products Joseph and his sons had made over the years became close friends. When Joseph died and went to heaven, many of these dear friends came to join the family and give condolences.

Jesus and his brothers discussed that things will be different now that Joseph has gone to heaven. Life will change greatly now for Mary and the rest of the children still at home. They all had that calm assurance of heaven and God the Father who has always been a part of their lives as a Jewish family. Many relatives and special friends from Bethlehem came to Nazareth and each one was such a strength, Grace, Diane, Elias, Shahir, Rajade, Bashir, Fadi, Riad, Adel, and Rafiq. They had so many fond memories growing up as cousins visited on the many adventures to Jerusalem.

Draw your own picture below:

Thirty

Time passed and two of my brothers had taken over the carpentry shop. All the girls were still caring for Mother and they were all working together to keep the animals, fields, and shop going. My wonderful childhood is behind me. My brothers and sisters and I get together often and laugh, reflect, and discuss what we are hearing from Jerusalem and from Rome and other parts of the world.

We still have many travelers stopping by and we learn what is happening in other towns. The travelers of late continue asking whether we are going to the festival in Jerusalem. We have gone every year and this year was no different even though Father Joseph was not with us. We began preparing for a journey to go to the festival.

While in Jerusalem I began teaching those who would listen from the steps of the synagogue. I taught lessons of life from the scrolls; I could see that those listening were very interested, and they asked me questions and I answered from learned knowledge or from the Heavenly Father. Each day more and more people came to hear me speak of this wisdom. Over the years I became close to some and they were all in attendance.

Since my brothers were taking care of the carpentry shop I knew I did not have to return. James had spoken to me about going to Joppa so James and I said goodbye to the family and left for Joppa from Jerusalem. Per our custom, we stopped to see Simon the Tanner and he ensured that the family will have everything we need for winter.

***

Mr. Titus, a friend of my father's, came by with sheep and we had a nice visit about my dad and how we all missed him. Mr. Titus had a sheep dog who did all the work, taking the sheep out to pasture, tending them and returning them home in the evening. Mr. Titus said, "If your dad was still with us he would get you a sheep dog." Mr. Titus said, "I am going to tell you a secret. My dog is going to have puppies and you can have one in two months." I told the family that night at dinner and there was such excitement, we could hardly wait to have our own dog. Mom said we could build it a house out of stone and left-over tiles for the roof and she would build the dog its own bed-bag.

Time passed, and Mr. Titus was a man of his word. He came carrying a little fur bundle in his arms. We all gathered around to pet this little puppy, it was so cute.

Mr. Titus handed the dog to Mom for inspection. He said it was a boy. Mom said, "It is your dog kids and now he is part of the family." Mr. Titus said he would be around to help train him to be a good sheep dog in a couple months when he is a bit bigger.

The family was trying to think of a good sheep-dog name. John said he liked the name Jake and the puppy put up his ears like he did too. Jake's tail began wagging and we all agreed, Jake it was.

Jake's feet grew to be huge and we were worried but Mr. Titus said, "it's okay, no worry, it is just the way dogs grow, feet first then ears." Jake was licking Mr. Titus' feet and he began laughing and we all joined in laughing at a weird and cute puppy behavior.

Jake learned fast that Mother was the one that would keep scraps for him. Jake loved fish scraps best and would eat anything except Zata.

The day arrived when Mr. Titus came to help us train Jake to listen and do what we said and Jake was a fast learner. Mr. Titus taught him to sit, wait, be nice, roll over, go get the lambs, easy, come back, go left, go right, go fast, and stop. The best one he learned was to "get Mother." He would go to the door of the house and bark until she came out. Mrs. Titus made special puppy treats Mom would give him.

Jake became more valuable to our family every day, he was a true protector. He always seemed to get between us and danger. Jake could tell who was a good person, and who was a bad person and would warn us with the way he greeted them. He had better discernment than many people I knew. He seemed to know all of Father's friends even though he had never met them.

Jake learned to jump over the fence where we kept the lambs but he could not get over the goat pen. Dad had made us make it higher to keep the goats in the pen and out of trouble. Jake just seemed to want to play with Giant as he would go to the fence if Giant was near. We decided to take Giant and Jake to the field to play in the freshly cut hay. When we told Mom where we would be she said if we made a mess of the stack of hay we had to fix it before we left for home.

This day was a first for Jake and Giant. They became the best of friends. They ran and jumped and butted heads until Jake got tired of a sore head. Jake began nipping at Giant's tail and Giant would try to see what Jake was nipping at but couldn't and went in circles. Then Jake tried to get on Giant's back and after a few tries Giant let him. Giant would then let him ride everywhere he went.

***

We planned to take Jake with us for his first big walk of 70 miles to Bethany to meet Lazarus, Mary, and Martha and some of my friends. On the way we made a stop at Galilee to visit the fishermen who looked to be having great catches. The fishermen gave Jake many fish treats. Jake wasn't sure about the water, so John picked up a stick just like the one we taught him to fetch with at home and when John hurled it into the water Jake jumped right in and swam back with it in his mouth. The smells and sites kept him busy until we left.

We arrived at Ein Karen at supper time and added our food to theirs. Jake got to meet Aunt Elizabeth and Jake took to her like a bear to honey and she felt the same about him. She said "I always wanted a dog but living in a village we had no need. Jake will you be my friend, and can we visit each other?" Jake looked up at her with his big brown eyes and assured her by wagging his tail that they were best of friends.

Thirty-one

Jesus was in the synagogue at Nazareth and was reading the scripture of Isaiah. Jesus spoke to the people, "Today this scripture has been fulfilled in your hearing of it." Jesus taught others and was loved and praised by all in attendance. Jesus conducted teachings in many synagogues and was recognized, honored, and praised by many around the region.

Jesus came back to Nazareth where he had been brought up and entered the synagogue as was his custom on the Sabbath day. He stood up to read and was handed a scroll from the prophet Isaiah. He opened it where it was written in Isaiah 61:1-3.

> The spirit of the Lord is upon me because he anointed me, the anointed one, the messiah to preach the good news, the gospel, too the poor. He has sent me to announce release to the captives and recovery of sight to the blind. He sent me forth as delivered, those who are oppressed, downtrodden, bruised, crushed, and broken down by calamity to proclaim the accepted and acceptable year of the Lord. The day when salvation and the free favor of God profusely abound.

Jesus rolled up the scroll and gave it back to the attendant. "Who is this Jesus?" People answer "The carpenter's son. Healer, savior, judge and king. A man of prayer and full of grace. He prays everywhere, in the hills, tombs, tables, rivers, homes, and in the open air." One woman shouted out "Things he says cannot save, it is God who will not fail us."

***

Things seem to be different. There is a special atmosphere around Nazareth. Many people began to come to Galilee to gather around Jesus to ask questions and to hear what Jesus was planning to do as he left family and friends to do the Heavenly Father's will. Jesus had many friends around the Galilee. Not one knew the future for Jesus or why they felt so strongly to follow him as he set out to do his Heavenly Father's will. The people he would meet along the way came to him for prayer, to be healed and to be set free from the powers of darkness. They saw Jesus with the power to cast out demons from those who had suffered many years. Yes the blind could see, the lame could walk, and many were raised from the dead. He fed 5000 people with two fish and five loaves and had twelve baskets of leftovers. This happened on a hillside of the Galilee.

People listened to Jesus teach them from a boat while they were on the shore of the Galilee. Jesus had many friends who were fishermen who liked to hear him when he taught about the scriptures and it was always more than what the rabbi and cantor taught. Jesus spoke with a deeper understanding and performed many miracles around Galilee.

Complete the picture of the boat below.

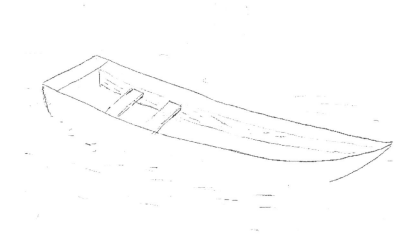

Thirty-two

Jesus reflects that it has been several years since his father joined the Heavenly Father in Heaven. The girls have done well, and several are married and the boys are all in a trade and doing well and are seeking wives. They remain faithful to Mother and family still at home. When I went back to Nazareth we sat around the table discussing the wonderful stories in each of our lives and how we were truly blessed each day. Mother Mary's friends came to our house often for prayer. They all discussed their children and talked of marriage plans for the girls.

Jesus had made chests for all the girls and they were preparing their dowries. Just for fun, Jesus put a hammer handle and a stir stick in each chest. Jesus also put other things they would need for their own homes. As olive wood made such wonderful bowls brother Simon made each one their own set. Each brother also included a useful gift such as hand carved cups. Many young men from near and afar had heard about the carpenter's daughters and how they could read and write and were filled with wisdom and knew how to do many tasks such as helping with the flocks and some of these men traveled to meet them.

***

I noticed that Boaz is getting too old to do work but we cannot let him go. He has helped Barley make many new donkeys and we have three new female donkeys right now.

***

Jesus had made many friends throughout his lifetime from Dan to Bathsheba. These friends became his disciples such as Mathias, Peter, John, Matthew, Judas, Thomas, Andrew, Judas, Nathanael, and many women in his life followed him. Mary, his mother, Anna, Ruth, Samaia, Rachel, Delilah, and many of his friends from Magdala including Mary Magdalene.

***

I had learned many lessons from our cantor, rabbi, and heroes of faith. My favorites are Noah, Moses, Samson, Daniel, David, and many others. The rabbi had made sure we knew the commandments. There were the big ten and hundreds of others. The rabbi taught us much about the food and how we were to prepare it and how to eat it and why it was important to follow the laws. I began to see more miracles in my life among the people. Blind eyes could see, dead people came back to life, the lame could walk, and tax-collectors stopped cheating.

An elder says "Jesus gives great blessings to all the places he goes." He brings comfort, mercy, and hope from the God in Heaven he calls Father. He speaks of the coming Pentecost and Repentance and that heaven is waiting. Jesus also speaks of the sin (the yeast of the Pharisees) and the place called hell. It has been said Jesus has been baptized in the Jorden River by his cousin John the Baptist from An Karen.

***

On my last day in Nazareth there was an order brought to the carpentry shop for 500 Mezuzahs and to have Deuteronomy 6:4-9 placed inside each one. There was also an order for basic menorahs. We had made them out of wood from the forest over the years and now many people desire them.

We also had orders for scroll handles and they wanted them made of hard-wood from Lebanon. My brothers were also making many gifts out of scrap wood for Purim. We also had a new order for stools. My brothers had it all under control. Now the day came when I went to Jerusalem for the last time. I went to the temple to find the rabbi and meet with some of the elders for a time of talking together about the deep feelings I was having. I had had some dreams and visions that concerned me for the people both Jews and Gentiles. There was a man that came to me and spoke kindly to me in the temple. Jesus said, "I felt like I had known him all my life." The man said, "I am Lazarus from Bethany." I said, "Have we ever met before? Lazarus replied, "Not really but I have known you from a distance since we were young boys. You spoke to and with the scholars and elders on the temple steps and I was there listening to all you had to teach us. Now I want to invite you to my home as long as you will be in Jerusalem. It is almost dinner time and you can eat with us and meet my sisters Martha and Mary. They are both widows and have been left with a villa and a large house with room for travelers."

When we arrived at the gate the keeper who was also the gardener let us enter this most lovely garden. We walked by the millstone where the donkeys were turning it making grain into flour. The smell was wonderful. Then Lazarus said "Come, I will show you the wine press." It had just pressed ripened grapes that day.

He said we will enjoy a cup of last year's wine from a pot in the house. Then we went into a large room and another millstone was filled with olives to be pressed early the next day. Many clay jars with lids were ready to be filled. Then we walked out of the olive press room and I saw many jars with salted olives being prepared for the Passover feast. The oil lanterns were lit in the porch area where we would be served the evening meal.

As we came to the porch Martha and Mary were sitting in silence. When they saw us walking toward them they immediately stood up and began to prepare the food and water. Everything was ready to serve when we got to the house. I had never been in such a large villa with so many luxuries. When I was a boy there was no way just one family in our village would have all of these things. Mary was first to greet us. Mary was full of questions, she had heard from a friend that I was in the temple; I was known as a teacher and miracles happened as I prayed for the people with the Heavenly Father who answered the prayers.

Martha went to the oven and took out the fresh bread she had ready for the morning. She brought us fresh leben, the best I had had in a long time. She served olives, fresh garlic, lemons, boiled eggs, and tasty herbs along with the bread. I was really hungry and I was blessed because they kept bringing more food. I could see that the comments I made to Martha about the good food and the peace I felt in her garden pleased her. Every room we visited had a special presence, it was all very comfortable. She was so busy I don't know if she really heard all I said. Martha was a bit upset with Mary who was not being a help. She just wanted to sit and listen to Lazarus and me talking. She wants to be taught. She is very bright and asked good questions of me.

Jesus shared what the Lord had spoken of for him to do in the future. Very shortly friends from Bethany saw the lamp in the porch and Martha scurrying around and they came and joined Jesus, Lazarus, and Mary and the teaching Jesus was giving. Martha continued to prepare and serve food. Mary sat with her friends and learned about new scriptures and learned about dreams and visions. Jesus felt right at home in Bethany. He felt wanted, needed, and accepted by this new-found family. Jesus felt strongly that this would be his new home away from home. He was loved and cared for in every way. His stay in Bethany was so restful, peaceful, and most prayerful by all the family, friends, and neighbors.

When I left Bethany, I knew I would return for refreshing times in the years ahead. Each time I returned Mary and Martha had a gift for me. The last was a new robe of fine woven cloth without one seam. They had made me a woolen prayer shawl out of the wool from their own sheep. When they saw that my sandals needed repair they went to the leather shop and had new winter sandals made for me.

Jesus thanked them over and over and his Heavenly Father for his gift of friendship for all the love he had received from his new-found family. He prayed for all of the folks in Bethany with just a great big "Thank you Lord" for each person and he looked up into the sky to his Heavenly Father, "They have been such a blessing to me, truly a gift from you. Father always please let me be a blessing to my friends. I knew it was now time to be completely about my Father's business.

Thirty-three

I am one of Jesus' sisters, Salome. I miss having my big brother Jesus at home. As long as I can remember I looked up to Jesus and he always had the answers to my questions. Jesus has stayed close to each of us as we grew up in our home in Nazareth. We saw the compassion he had for everyone and he placed in our hearts a desire to do the same.

My life will remain in Nazareth and some of my brothers and sisters have made plans to build homes here also. Sometimes I have the uneasy feeling that the plans Father God has for Jesus will totally change our family. Mother stays so close to him these days and follows him as he goes to Jerusalem and visits family and friends. Many people from the Galilee are coming more and more to listen to Jesus' teaching and just to have him touch them in prayer.

Jesus also prays for those not able to come in person because people believe that God hears his prayers. The reports around the Galilee is that Jesus is healing the sick, making the blind sea, making cripples walk, and bringing the dead alive. The reports of these miracles are talked about as far away as Jerusalem. The fishermen that have been our friends all our lives are now talking like Jesus. John the Baptist our cousin has always been a leader and now has thousands of followers who have been baptized for the remission of sin.

Jesus has appointed twelve to be his personal disciples. Jesus told us all about the place called heaven and how his cousin John was baptizing people in the Jordan River for the remission of sin. We listened intently as he read books on heaven and eternal life. Jesus told us of his vision of heaven and how he saw Joseph our dad, who is in heaven.

I never saw Jesus as excited as he was when he told us and our friends about heaven and all the angels around the throne of God the Heavenly Father.

Jesus had so much to teach us and he said "So little time." He said, "One day we will all see God and our home in heaven is waiting for us." I remember the day he sat with me and explained how I never had to fear death. He explained where fear comes from and how I can take my stand against the devil and all the fallen angels on earth.

My dear loving brother, today is about the Heavenly Father's business and he is showing others like he showed me, all of heaven is prepared and waits for us to come one day. Jesus told me that heaven has a big yard and is big enough for all the children to play.

I hear that there is negative talk about Jesus which surprises me as Jesus has only meant good for others. They say he broke the law on the Sabbath, that he ate on that day and that he healed someone on that day which is considered work.

The faithful said he was the promised redeemer while others hated him without reason and many were false witnesses to misdeeds even though he was known for his righteousness.

The holiness of time and place was sensed by all who met Jesus. Jesus had an inner faith and understanding of scripture within him placed by the Holy Father making him aware of what the people needed to hear and apply to their lives. Little did they know they would become a part of the end moments of time in Jesus' life.

The miracles happened just like he said they would. His mother, family, friends, and disciples, and Mary Magdalene witnessed what were the last hours of his life. Peter denied him three times and Judas sold him out for 30 pieces silver.

After Jesus was arrested he was rejected when the question arose about who to release to freedom. Hecklers shouted "Barabbas, Barabbas" and Barabbas was freed leaving Jesus to die on the cross. There was much weeping because he was loved so deeply. He was given a new tomb and an angel was in charge over him. The two Marys went to the tomb to put spices on him and prepare him for burial. They reported back to Peter and all the friends hiding "He is alive, he is not in the tomb." He's alive, and I am forgiven, Heaven's gates are open wide.

The big question on everyone's mind is where do we go from here? They all said it is time to pray and seek guidance from the Heavenly Father, to let him speak to our hearts like he did to and for Jesus. We must take the good news to our world; people are waiting for us to come to them. Jesus taught us all how to plan an adventure, he always stopped along the way and taught people just like he did when we were at the synagogue.

The fond memories are all so real to us, you might say the memories are alive in our spirits like no other thoughts. Today we go on the adventure the Father had planned for us before time because we were obedient to the call. To go and tell that old story of Jesus and his love to a lost and dying world. Yes, we are ready for Jesus to come back and take us to a new heaven, a new Jerusalem, and a new earth. He has prepared a place for all of us and we will see Jesus for ever and ever. We are on the winning side. What a day that will be. We will all see Jesus. We are About the Father's business in this end hour because he came, we went, and because we went we will return, and He will say "well done my good and faithful children.

Meeting on the Galilee, Jesus said "Come follow me and I will make you fishers of men." Docking their boats, putting their nets in the hands of the next generation, many people followed him to Jerusalem. His mother Mary, Mary Magdalene, and many other women joined them.

Acts 1:9-11 Now when He had spoken these things, while they watched, He was taken up, and a cloud received Him out of their sight. And while they looked steadfastly toward heaven as He went up, behold, two men stood by them in white apparel, who also said, "Men of Galilee, why do you stand gazing up into heaven? This same Jesus, who was taken up from you into heaven, will so come in like manner as you saw Him go into heaven."

Mark 16:19&20 So then, after the Lord had spoken to them, He was received up into heaven, and sat down at the right hand of God. And they went out and preached everywhere, the Lord working with them and confirming the word through the accompanying signs. Amen.

Draw your own picture below:

What Others Thought

Leone's book really puts Jesus' childhood in a historical perspective. I liked how Jesus was learning from the priests; was a brother; played in the carpentry shop and created things. In the book, the child Jesus had a strong connection to God.

Even though these are fictional stories, Leone has gone to the towns in this book many times and has put her heart into the book, and that experience makes the stories seem vivid and real. This book makes learning about Jesus and His relationships fun and exciting – finding out about His rock collection and all of His explorations, naming all of His animals (chickens, goats and donkeys), and when He got into trouble and learning from everyone around Him.

The vocabulary in Leone's book is easy to understand even for the little ones, and it's a lot of fun learning about the exciting adventures and following Jesus through life from age 5 to 33. These stories will hook you in until the end. When I see Jesus one day, I know He will want to play outside with me.

Sophie, age 11

***

Leone has been an inspiration to me and has also been big part in my journey of faith. She has set an amazing example for me to look up to. Around thirty-five years ago, she came to speak at my church to my Grandma and they have been close friends ever since.

This book shows Jesus' childhood in a new perspective. I don't know of any children's books or any books in fact that tell the story of His childhood. Although these stories are fiction, Leone helps us glimpse at what it may have been like for Jesus growing up. In reading this book, Leone has made me want to investigate further. We know of the Christmas story and twelve year old Jesus talking to the temple officials. Sadly, we know very little about the rest of Jesus' childhood, but this collection of short stories helps clear some of those questions for me.

When you read the Bible it is all about adults, there is very little about children. One of my favorite parts of the book is learning how they lived 2000 years ago. I love how easy the stories are to read and how it shows that Jesus was fully human. They also make great bedtime stories for kids. My favorite story is about the sandstorm when they had to wait out the storm inside with all the baby chicks. Also, the stories are in chronological order starting at age five until thirty-three. Most importantly, I like how these stories are inspired by Leone's twenty-three trips to the Holy Land.

Elise, age 14

***

. I found this book fun to read and for young children and teens. This book offers readers a picture of what Jesus' young life could have been like. He experienced life as a human just like us and increased in wisdom and knowledge from his human experience and experience with the Heavenly Father. Having known Leone for over 40 years I know she has travelled extensively in Israel and has walked many of the same places in the Holy Land where Jesus lived and visited. I would give this book to my grandchildren to give them another picture of life in the time of Jesus. It would also be a wonderful book for Sunday school teachers to teach life lessons about caring for family, neighbors, and pets. I hope you will enjoy this book and share it with the children in your life.

- Ann LaGrange

Story Support

The human side of Jesus has always been of interest to me. I spent quite a bit of time in the Middle East and in Israel from Dan to Bathsheba. I have had many wonderful times of fellowship exploring with local people, building a garden in The Fields of Boaz, walking the narrow streets of the villages, climbing the hills up to Nazareth, drinking from the ancient well of Mary (Mary's well), buying fruit and fresh flatbread in the market place, picking olives, and going to the olive press.

I also have stopped to play ball with the children in the streets and I envisioned that they looked like Jesus and his family had looked. I wandered around the churches, visited Mary's family home, and went to the edge of the hill looking over the Valley of Megiddo knowing more wars have been fought on that piece of ground than anywhere else in the world and that the last battle will be fought right there.

I have recently visited Nazareth Village with my friend Barbara, Dvora Maor, Tour guide, and some Messianic Jewish friends. All the adults in the village were in historically accurate costumes and it felt like I stepped back in time. It looked just like Jesus and his family would have looked 2000 years ago. It made my heart sing to see how simple and hard life was at that time.

I was thinking "no wonder Jesus was coming back, he wants to show us how to live by his example." I was living in a moment of time that had gone backwards just for me. On that special day in Nazareth Village, the idea for this book came back to my thoughts from many years earlier and I knew I would complete this work.

***

From the Bible and supporting historical information, I learned that Joseph was a very good and godly man and he and Mary lived within Jewish laws and traditions. God chose them to raise his son Jesus in the land of Israel. Mary was told what name to give Jesus and Joseph was told by an angel of the Lord in a dream about the Holy Spirit that came upon Mary and conceived the child Jesus in her womb.

This was a lot to receive and believe. However, Joseph knew that it was God speaking to him and understood the message. Joseph chose to wed Mary and be the earthly Father to Jesus and many other boys and girls in their big family. It was common for Jewish families to have a new baby every year.

Joseph was faithful and full of wisdom and knowledge and creative in his professions of carpentry and masonry. Joseph could design and build a family home from stone with wooden doors and wooden window frames with or without Roman glass from the ships at Ashdod. In addition to all forms of carpentry, one of his specialties was large sand-ovens with baked clay lids.

Each year Joseph would take the family to Jerusalem for festivals. He would take two doves and many pigeons. Joseph built bird cages large enough to transport chickens and would bring newly designed masonry tools and carpentry tools and devices for others to create tools, wheels, and other items. He would show his newest inventions to the elders and friends he would meet at the city gates along the way and at the temple among men from other villages.

Joseph would have taught his children, and especially Jesus as he was the first born. Additionally Jesus would have helped with the other children in many ways. During visits to Simon the tanner, Simon would have provided instruction in leather tanning and crafting, fish drying, and information about how to barter with the ships in the port of Ashdod on the big sea. Joseph said to Jesus, "Simon is righteous and devout, he loves our land.

He, like you, has a spiritual understanding about the signs of the times."

Jesus became creative like Simon and his earthly father Joseph and was able to create many new things. Joseph told him "If you can think it you can build it." Joseph would have taught Jesus and all the boys how to care for animals and how to prepare the family for travel when going to Ein Gedi, Joppa, Jerusalem, Jericho, Bethlehem, Galilee, and other places to meet family, friends, teachers, and strangers at the gates.

Jesus had many joyful times during his childhood with his family, friends, and while on adventures with his family. Jesus knew he had a Heavenly Father and Jesus regularly had insight into who he was and what his life was going to be like in the future. When he was a teenager and young adult, Jesus' friends included Peter, James, John, Mary Magdalene, Andrew, Simon, and many others. They knew something was different about him, desired to be with him, and later wrote about him.

Jesus was in communication with the Heavenly Father frequently and had a deep desire to see people healed, to see people being loving towards each other, taking care of each other, and living godly lives. He was drawn to help widows, orphans, the poor, and strangers.

He always found time to be helpful. Jesus had great compassion and his love was unconditional.

Note: There are church doctrines that say Jesus had no brothers and sisters, however, the scriptures state he did. There is also no support for Jesus being violent or destructive as a child. Jesus had an inner knowing of who he was and a hunger to learn the scriptures. He had the gift of teaching even as a twelve year-old. He could read and write at an early age but never wrote a book...that we know of.

***

One of the things I noticed in Israel was that people, roads, and things were often named after each other such as the Damascus road named after the town, Mary Magdalen's last name from the town of Magdala, and the town of Dothan named after the first family that lived there. I continued this tradition in many of the stories.

Many of the adventures or experiences depicted in these stories I learned from the Holy Bible, historical information, and my 23 visits to walk where Jesus walked over 2000 years ago. Each time I visited Nazareth, Bethlehem, the Galilee, and Capernaum I felt the presence of the Lord. On one trip to a town called Nain, a group of children were outside playing with a worn out ball and I bought that ball for ten dollars so they could buy a new one. I took the worn ball on the bus with me for the rest of the trip. I thought the kids looked like Jesus would have when he was young and playing on the streets of Nazareth.

    I was blessed to be part of the Messianic Jewish tour group for ten days, five of which were spent in Nazareth. The Nazareth village was open to the public and was maintained just as it would have been in Jesus' time. The stories in this book that you read to little ones were birthed in Nazareth. I have placed Jesus with his earthly family doing what kids did at that time. Joseph was a teacher and one who would have taken Jesus, his brothers, sisters, and wife Mary on many adventures. Jesus learned at the temple and at the city gates from the elders, rabbis, cantors, and many of Father Joseph's friends. Simon the Tanner, at Joppa on the big sea was also a very close friend to Joseph and his family.

Afterward

The rest of the story is for you and I to take lessons to our world following Jesus' example and to share scripture from the Holy Bible. Like Jesus taught his disciples, he will teach you and others.

Trust in the Lord for our future. The stories in this book took place more than 2000 years ago. People can still find hope, joy, peace, and happiness from the same stories and lessons Jesus learned and taught from when he was here on earth. My hope is that this book creates a lasting interest in Jesus Christ, his salvation, and his teaching.

Contact Information

You may contact me at leoneaj38@gmail.com for:

- Speaking engagements
- Seminars
- Retreats
- Teaching and training
- Book signing events
- Radio Interviews
- Outreach for children

Additionally, this book is available through Amazon.com and other booksellers.

Boaz and Barley

Made in the USA
Columbia, SC
26 May 2021